secret of the round tower

Random House/New York

secret of the round tower

by ANNE SINCLAIR WILLIAMS

drawings by J.C. KOCSIS

Acknowledgments

My grateful thanks to Mr. Jay Williams for his suggestions and help with medieval details; to Mme. Viviane Andral of Sarlat, France, for checking data on Guyenne; to Mme. Espinoze for allowing me access to the Sarlat Public Library; to "King," prototype of the Fur Knight; and to Shepard Odell whose *The Lore of the Unicorn* was an invaluable source.

—Anne Sinclair Williams

Copyright ©1968 by Anne Sinclair Williams

All rights reserved under International and Pan-American Copyright Conventions. Published in the United States by Random House, Inc., New York, and simultaneously in Canada, by Random House of Canada Limited, Toronto.

Library of Congress Catalog Card Number: 68-23651

Manufactured in the United States of America

To David Huntington Williams
and Mark Philip Baughan with love

Foreword

To people of the Middle Ages, the unicorn was real. In western Europe, he was thought to have the body of a horse. Others said he was the shape and build of a goat. Everyone agreed, however, that from his forehead grew a single horn and that the unicorn himself was a creature of remarkable powers always and often, of extraordinary beauty.

There is a part of southwest France where prehistoric caves and ancient castles abound, a land so alive with history and legend that the past seems more real than the present and no tale seems too unlikely to have happened.

It is unicorn country....

The Fur Knight

The May sun caressed Galpin's new heaume and likewise his new armor, both of which he had donned for the first time. In his hand, as he practiced strokes, in the cobblestoned courtyard, glistened a sword.

"You are not to use a real sword yet with no knight around and you know it!" his sister Melisande cried. She peered down from the narrow window of the East Tower. From this vantage point she could see Galpin pause and breathe hard. "Papa says you are too young to go to Châteauroc yet; he says fourteen is quite young enough to start learning to be a squire. And both our parents say you did poorly as page to the Comte de Mireau."

This was a slight exaggeration. Melisande had overheard her father and the count laughing over some prank of Galpin's while her mother protested she did not think it especially amusing.

"Papa says I too shall have a horse of my own," yelled Melisande.

"Did I ever say you would not?" So intent was Galpin on the practice of sword-play that he did not trouble to raise his voice. In his new armor and with the man-sized sword he was as handsome as a real knight, and it was easy indeed to picture him riding to war beside his father and the Sire de Châteauroc's peers. Ride to battle they would, to fight the English, pennons waving and bugles blowing, while Melisande and Maman supervised the Château de Vrillac staff, sewed, spun, embroidered, and discussed

ways to decorate the new round tower. One floor of it was all to be Melisande's—but what is a new round tower compared to a horse of one's own? And who would not prefer to ride armorclad to battle rather than oversee a lot of servants?

"I said you did poorly as page!" She screamed this time as loudly as she could.

"Silence, you stupid sister!" Galpin removed the heaume with eye-slits the better to glare at her. "We are related to the Count as we are to other nobles. What is a little water in the armor among family? And as for my staying home awhile, it is because Papa wishes me to benefit from the finest tutoring in the arts of chivalry to be found. And the best tutors are right here."

"Well, I think pouring water over the armor was stupid and unoriginal," Meli said. "Life is a serious matter and your lord might have needed that armor and it would have been all rusted."

Galpin smiled. "That fast? Little do you know of armor, Meli. But I will tell you a secret I have told no one: I had had a few sips of wine."

"So you were drunk!" She yelled again. "How can you ever take the vows of knighthood, Galpin? One must promise never to get drunk, ever, ever, ever. Why, even I know that and I am only a girl."

"And a cross and disagreeable one at that. Meli, it is not my fault you can never be a knight or that Papa has given Tonnerre to me. Women cannot be knights; they become ladies." He paused. "Some of them. As for Tonnerre, you would never be strong enough to ride him. Here! Here! Get out of my way, Bayard!"

Galpin had moved almost beyond Melisande's vision. Almost, but not quite. She saw him raise the sword high to keep the Great Pyrenee from harm's way. He raised it none too soon. The huge dog, snow-white and almost as large as a full-grown bear, had jumped and snapped at the sword, his teeth clicking against the metal blade. When his forepaws hit the ground, the fur on his chin was stained red.

"Bayard!"

Melisande sped down the corridor, through the Middle Hall, down the East Tower's winding stairs. When she reached the courtyard, Galpin was cradling Bayard's head in his arm and Bayard was licking Galpin's face. It was drained of color and there were tears in Galpin's eyes, some of which trickled down the side of his nose, unheeded.

"He is unharmed, Meli. It is nought but a slight cut, thank God." Galpin swallowed. "He thought it was my practice sword, not a real one. I have never used a real one before in his presence. Oh Bayard, my Bayard bold and brave, never would I forgive myself if I had hurt you badly! I am so sorry."

Again the wet tongue swept the boy's face; Bayard raised his massive head and butted his master gently under the chin. Melisande sat down. She patted the thick white fur and was rewarded with a low moan and a lick. "Beautiful Bayard! The best! The finest! The one Fur Knight!" She kissed the soft place between the eyes. "He moans with love, Galpin, just as he used to when he was little. Do you remember?"

"Who could forget? Meli, the cut still bleeds. You know more of herbs than I, and how to stanch a wound...."

With a swish of her long skirts to keep from tripping on them, Meli rose to her feet. "Lilies are best for blade wounds. Wait here. There is a patch of lily-of-the-valley the other side of the drawbridge. I hope they will do. And I must fetch some wine in which to soak them."

In no time, Meli was back. She and Galpin took turns pressing

7

the wine-soaked lilies against the cut. Bayard sighed blissfully and rolled his eyes. Meli began to chant:

"Our Bayard bold, and brave, and white, we dub thee now the One Fur Knight," Galpin finished along with her. "Oncle Geoffroi said that was the finest knighting ceremony he had ever come upon unexpectedly, and that my couplet was magnificent. You were so small you could hardly hold Bayard, he was such a big and plump puppy. My toy sword missed his shoulder and hit him on the nose. Dear Oncle Geoffroi; I did love him so." Galpin removed the pressure from the cut and studied it. No blood appeared. "Meli, you have healed the Fur Knight. He is well again. Thank you."

She nodded. "Did you hear about that kitten he rescued last week? Cook says it will live. That makes the third wee beast he has brought home since Candlemas. He really is a fur knight and next to Papa I love him best, even if he does belong to you. And I shall love my horse more than anyone. Oh, when am I to be given my horse?"

"Truly, I do not know. When you become a lady-in-waiting, or perhaps be..." Footsteps rang against the cobblestones. "Oh, confound it!" Galpin said. "It is my chess tutor and he will come looking if I do not go quickly. How I detest that game!" He reached for the sword and stared at his sister. "I took it from the armory when no one was about."

"All right. I will put it back for you." The promise would be worth whatever the cost, for now Galpin would give her a treat in exchange. And a big one it would be today, nothing less than a ride with Galpin on Tonnerre through The Forest before sundown.

8

"…by the big walnut tree when the sun is over the keep," Galpin was saying. "Do not forget!"

As if she could, Meli thought, as she watched her brother and the chess tutor step into the North Hall where the games were kept. It would be a long day before Galpin could keep his promise; there would be his law tutor after this one, then the jousting lesson which he so loved, followed by magic and then lunch…. boys studied such wonderful subjects. At least Maman had taught her to read and write.

The Story of Oncle Geoffroi

The sun was a long way yet from the chapel tower. Beside Melisande, Bayard lay in a wide, white heap, with his nose resting between his forepaws and his eyes closed. Sensing her gaze, he opened the eye nearest to her and growled tenderly. Meli scrambled to her feet and hastened to the armory. She managed to replace the sword unobserved, so busy was the château staff with early morning chores. When she returned to the courtyard, one of the serfs dropped a stone from the nearly-completed new round tower. Its clatter so startled Meli that she gave a little cry. Then she smiled up at the man with the emptied hands and terrified eyes. She waved reassuringly.

"Melisande," her mother called down, "I will not have you in the courtyard while the men are building. You know that and you know why. You might have been killed."

"Yes, Maman."

"Have you chosen your design yet?"

"Yes. I am going to embroider a unicorn." Meli's eyes shone. "I have practiced the drawing of it, and it is well done, Maman. Oh Maman, will you please tell me the story once more, the story of Oncle Geoffroi and the unicorn in The Forest?"

"If you will come inside and set to work."

For what seemed a long time, Maman stared at the canvas on which Meli's unicorn was sketched. As she did so, Meli shifted from one foot to the other.

"But this is excellent, my darling. Truly." Maman's voice was soft, low, and wondering.

Meli looked at the drawing and forgot, as she had not been able to do before, that she was its creator. It *was* excellent. Her unicorn was not pictured from a distance and from the side, with his body half-hidden by foliage and his eyes staring straight ahead so that their expression could not be seen, as in Oncle Geoffroi's painting. Her unicorn was caught in the act of turning as he leapt, four hoofs off the ground, his head following the thrust of his body so that the eyes stared straight at the onlooker. How many hours had Meli spent sketching the horses in the meadow and in the stables? Enough hours to acquire fair mastery in the drawing of a horse in motion. And as for Oncle Geoffroi's painting, she could see its every detail whenever she closed her eyes if such was her will. She had worked so hard and so long that when the time came to select a pose, the need to do so was past. Her unicorn appeared to her complete with horse's body twisting as he leapt, the tall single horn that grew from his forehead rising in a straight ivory spiral. Not a black spiral, as in Oncle Geoffroi's painting, but a white one. And she had found it necessary to shift the branch of the tree behind so that it formed a right angle to the ivory horn. It looked better that way.

Maman liked the fact that he was looking directly at the observer. "The eyes are good, Meli. But I cannot tell their color exactly; what is it?"

"I do not know. Sometimes I think they are the color of dark olives like Bayard's, sometimes the color of moss. What did Oncle Geoffroi say?"

"He never did. The unicorn he saw was far away like the one he painted. Moreover, the sun was in your uncle's eyes."

"Tell me the story again, please."

"It was a good twenty years ago, when your uncle was a mere youth, that he took a walk in The Forest...." Maman paused to change thread, picking one dipped in the purple dye she and Meli had mixed together the day before. "...in The Forest," she repeated, "all by himself. The sun was setting and..."

"Behind the keep, Maman. The sun was setting behind the keep."

Maman smiled. "The sun was setting behind the keep and your uncle was beyond the clearing, having passed the biggest walnut trees, and he was heading for our stream to water his horse. Suddenly the creature stopped and neighed."

"Softly," Meli added.

"...neighed softly. Your uncle said the air was full of gentle sound, almost a melody, and that small triumphant blasts came in

11

particular from the lilies-of-the-valley near that big rock you and Galpin used as a fort when you were little. On the rock's over-hang a nightingale perched, singing a song of such piercing beau-ty that Geoffroi shivered. The ferns swayed in rippling notes like those of the harp, and those notes were tossed into a different order by our stream. Underneath, the moss gave forth a deep, continuous rumble."

Maman paused, waiting for Meli's question. Meli hugged her knees hard.

"Was Oncle Geoffroi afraid?"

"Terrified. He stood as still as the rock itself. Something com-pelled him to turn his head and look at that gap between the trees. The sun had slipped not only behind the keep, but behind the far hills. The afterglow was fading fast and the plants had ceased their singing. Then it was bright again; he had to blink. Through the intense light, he saw the unicorn. His body was partly hid-den by the foliage but his black horn was brilliant in the light and all about him there was what your uncle called 'a kind of glow.' Geoffroi crossed himself and bowed. The unicorn turned his head, lowered it very slowly and with great courtesy, then leapt off into The Forest."

Maman carefully selected a new thread of Toulouse pastel blue. From the court, a servant girl could be heard raising her voice in argument until the cook's harsh command brought stillness.

"He bowed back," Meli said. "The unicorn bowed back to my Oncle Geoffroi."

"Yes, my child. And what a marvelous moment it must have been."

Discovery in the Forest

The Château de Vrillac was never more beautiful than at sunset. The golden light danced on the pointed, cone-shaped roof of the new round tower, warmed the yellow stone of walls and battlements, played hide-and-seek among the crenellations. As for the moat, it was a liquid diamond. Seen from above and at this hour, the castle was a fairy thing, perched high on the spur below, with the Murmurante River meandering off to the left, and the castles of Mireau and Châteauroc each in its eyrie on the neighboring ridged hills.

Galpin and Meli, astride Tonnerre, had paused to admire the view.

"The new tower is superb," Galpin said. "I prefer it to the old square ones we have."

"And Maman says I can have one whole floor for a bedroom all my own. Is that not wonderful?"

"You are indeed a favored girl." Galpin patted Tonnerre on his glossy black neck. The stallion nickered.

"He is beautiful," Meli said. She tightened her grip about her brother's waist and glanced down at the spot where Bayard had been lying beside them. Bayard was not there, only the imprint of his body on the grass.

"The Fur Knight has gone off, Galpin."

"He will return. Is not Tonnerre a marvel of a mount? I shall ride him up the stairs of your new tower to visit you if you would like it."

13

She laughed. Through the clearing, she could see their home as Papa had shown it to her when she stood no taller than Bayard on his four fur feet. It was the fairest sight in all Guyenne, and Oncle Geoffroi had surely said good-by to it before he rode off on his first and last Crusade. Papa had pointed out this view to her, and talked to her as if she were a grown woman. "A new wall here, a new tower there, but truly it does not change for all the improvements. We have stood here when we were your size, your Oncle Geoffroi and I, and our father before us, and his father before him, and so on, back in time. As Vrillac is a part of us, so are we a part of Vrillac."

Ours is the most beautiful château in all the world, thought Meli now as she and Galpin watched the sun slip from tower to hill. A breeze stirred the new green of the giant poplars that grew in the water-meadows by la Murmurante. The orange ball that was the sun could be stared at without squinting.

Loud barks came from the left. Bayard was bouncing up and down as if he were still in puppyhood, then running off to the thickest woods, then back to bark some more.

"Well! And what ails you, Sir Bayard?"

The dog stared back into his master's eyes and whined. He ran off to the woods again, then back to bark some more.

"Oh, all right. We shall come and see, shall we not, Meli? Hop down now."

She did as she was told. Galpin fastened Tonnerre to the biggest walnut tree, then set off after the dog. Bayard was silent as they moved, and Meli had a hard time keeping up with him and his master, they moved so fast. The breeze had died, leaving a great stillness behind. The air smelled deliciously of dampness and earth and, presently, of pine needles underfoot. Something crackled. A small creature stepping on a twig? An elf tripping? The forest teemed with secret life so that the silence itself seemed loud. Meli grabbed Galpin's hand. She thought she heard a steady rumbling from somewhere low, nearby, very close indeed. Right there where Bayard had flattened himself and was shivering, nose between his forepaws. He was as close to the overhang of the huge rock as one could get without actually crawling beneath.

"There, Meli. Where we used to play when we were small. There is something inside that the Fur Knight is guarding. See?"

Meli saw. Surely if Bayard were afraid he would not make

himself a sentinel, or would he? He was moaning softly and trembling from head to foot. For a moment Meli could not breathe for terror, and then she remembered: Bayard only moaned like that when he was happy. Moreover, his tail thumped hard against the ground as it would not do were he afraid. But how strange—with one of the thumps came the sound of a trumpet, incredibly soft, clear, triumphant.

"A trumpet?" said Galpin, his voice rising in mild surprise. "I must be dreaming." He stopped. "There, there, Bayard. Let me see what is inside."

Meli knelt and slid her hand also under the overhang. She was not afraid either. What harm could possibly befall them with Bayard so close by? But her hand shook slightly as it touched something warm and alive. She could tell it was living from the slight, steady throbbing that must be a heartbeat. A fawn? she wondered. Whatever the creature, it must be fragile indeed for its fur was the softest she had ever felt, as gentle to the touch as butterfly wings.

"Oh Galpin, how very soft it is!" She giggled. "It kissed me; it just kissed me on the back of the hand."

"The legs are very long, Meli. Be careful. We do not wish to hurt it, whatever it is."

Together they pulled, slowly and gently. The Fur Knight gave an enormous yawn, then lapsed into absolute stillness, head bowed. Again Meli heard rumbling. It was eerie but not unpleasant against what sounded for all the world like laughter from the brook. The laughter was the echo of pure joy, a sound she had only heard in dreams till now. The ferns rippled in answer and there was an unmistakable elfin blast from a blue bell. Just a little bit saucy, it sounded.

"Truly a perfect colt, the most perfect colt I have ever seen." Galpin's voice, huskier than usual, cut through the quiet. "I have never seen such a beautiful colt before in all my life."

His hand reached down to hip-level where the little creature's head reached. Pure white the foal was, and exquisitely formed with unusually long legs and large, luminous eyes that were a marvelous moss-green.

"A very new foal, Meli. So new he can barely stand."

Meli sat down and held out her arms. The foal moved instantly her way on wobbly long legs. It collapsed, head in her lap. She bent over to press her cheek against the thick white down. It was softer than Bayard's coat had ever been.

"Are you laughing or are you crying, Melisande?"

"I do not know; perhaps both. But I have found him, my very own, at last. My very own horse who is not a horse."

"What do you mean?"

"You cannot guess, Galpin? He is no horse, my little foal. He is a unicorn, a real, true unicorn!"

Meli's Very Own Foal

Meli lay in bed with her right arm separating the bed-curtains and her hand reaching until it touched the velvet softness of her foal. Awake, he would instantly respond by sniffing the palm of her hand with his muzzle. It was moist and cool like a freshly-fallen petal. Sometimes there would be a larger muzzle in her palm, and she would know that Bayard had roused himself to as-

21

sure her of his presence and that he was alertly on guard. He had appointed himself to this task, uttering moans of such dreadful volume and intensity when Galpin had tried to remove him from the foundling's presence that Galpin had been obliged to surrender.

"Silly Fur Knight! Must you always guard the smallest and most helpless? I thought you were mine." And he had cuffed his dog on the ear so gently that the fur did not even bend.

"How well-versed Bayard is in the Code of Chivalry," Papa had observed, and they had all laughed, so relieved were they to have it settled. For it had been a tiring fight. When Meli had insisted the little creature was a unicorn, both parents had denied it, pointing out the smoothness of the forehead.

"It grows in later, like teeth," Meli had explained.

Papa had replied she could not possibly know such a thing. Moreover, only last week the troubadors had sung of a dwarf whom King Arthur had met and whose infant son had been cared for by a female unicorn along with her own tiny young, each of whom already had an alicorn. "They are born with the horn, dear child," Papa had repeated.

"The next time the troubadors come, we shall have you with us to hear them sing of this knight. Shall we not, Louis?" Maman waited for Papa's nod of assent.

He pulled Meli close and smiled. "You will love it. You have always wanted to stay up for the troubadors. They describe the baby unicorns so vividly we listeners can almost see them."

"We can do far better than that right now, Papa. No 'almost' about it. We know what a baby unicorn looks like because I have one right here by my side. See?"

Her parents exchanged glances. "Darling, he is a most beautiful foal and I can understand that you love him." Papa cupped the foal's throat with his hand and the animal gazed up at him trustingly. His eyes were shining like dew before the sunlight had melted it away, Meli thought, or like the meadow pools after a rain. No wonder Papa stooped to plant a fleeting kiss upon the foal's neck. "You little beauty," he said. Then he kissed Meli. "My little beauties."

"Believe me, Papa, this is a real, true unicorn. I know it and so does Galpin. We heard the lilies trumpet and the moss rumbling."

Papa sighed and turned to Maman. "Blanche, your daughter has too much imagination or you tell stories too well."

"Speak of your brother, Louis. For who but he in this family has ever seen a unicorn?"

"I have, Maman."

"Me too," said Galpin.

"Be quiet, both of you!" Papa said in reproof. "I will not have you speak so to your mother. You compel me to tell you what Corbet reported: A dead mare was found not far from The Forest this afternoon. She had foaled, but her young was not to be found. A brace of disobedient children with a huge white dog discovered it later under the big rock."

Meli swallowed. A drop of wax slid down the candle by the door, slowly, very slowly. The light was blurred.

Papa spoke calmly now. He was telling her she could keep the foal until he grew big. "A charger is a man's steed, not a woman's,

23

and certainly not for a small girl. In time, you will have to accept a palfrey in his place. Is that understood?"

She nodded.

"It will be the prettiest one in all the land," Papa promised. Then he had kissed her.

Bayard had refused to be parted from his chosen charge and the family, laughing, had escorted Meli and the two white creatures to her room, Maman sending the squire Leon to fetch the servant girl, Nanette. "She will feed him during the night," Maman promised. "As for you, you are to sleep."

And now, with her hand on the foundling's neck, Meli watched as Nanette heated the milk over the dying fire.

"Is it ready?" Meli called. "He whimpers from hunger, the little darling. That's right, Bayard, kiss him."

"Ssshh! You are supposed to be asleep, my lady."

Nanette knelt by the bed and stroked both animals as Meli held the pewter cup. The room was dark but the creatures shone as if moonbeams were caught in their fur. The smaller had placed his head in her lap and ate noisily, with gusto.

"Nanette."

"Yes, my lady?"

"His name is Champion and he is my very own real, true unicorn."

"If my lady says so." Nanette reached for the emptied cup. "How he does shine in the dark, the small one, and the dog too! What a pretty pair the two of them make!"

Others thought so too. For at first, Bayard would not be parted from Champion. Wherever his charge went, Bayard followed, and whenever Champion needed rest—which was very often—there was always the bearlike fur against which to lean and cuddle. Meli remembered it well, a massive wall against which one could become nearly invisible and which could be relied upon to be ever and warmly present.

When Champion was less collapsible, Meli took him down to the courtyard where he and Bayard played. During these periods the big dog lost most of his clumsiness. He too would run and jump, and though Champion was the more graceful, it would be difficult to say which of the two gave the greater pleasure. At these times, the wrangling in the kitchen would stop, and much of the work as well, as Nanette or Lise yelled their report from the doorway to those inside who could not drop an urgent task to watch.

"Careful! Here he comes," Lise called. "Why, he is heading for the kitchen here. . . . but why on earth? . . ."

". . . to fetch his kitten!" a voice replied from inside. And sure enough, Bayard reappeared with the kitten in his mouth. He placed it at Champion's feet. They faced each other, the kitten staring out of eyes not too long opened. Meli waited for it to puff out like the fire bellows and make the hissing sound of fear. The animals touched noses. The kitten bowed its head and produced a small boiling sound only audible to those nearby. Arching its back, it rubbed against Champion's right leg. He leaned down and licked it from head to tail. The kitten sprang to one side,

25

Champion to the other, and they were off on some secret game of their own in which Bayard too took part. Finally, the kitten leaped on Champion's back and settled, paws kneading the slim neck, rather like Cook with a bowlful of dough.

The onlookers clapped. Within hours, there was not one member of the staff who did not drop all but the most pressing tasks to watch this show whenever it took place, and not one but that agreed it was better than anything the wandering minstrels could provide. Yet somehow the chores got done. Cook raised his voice in song, not scolding. The eldest servant girl lost her sour look and the lazy squire no longer shirked his job.

"Incredible, the way the animals love that colt," remarked Maman to her husband. "You should leave the hunt to watch them one day, Louis. You really should. The whole château is talking about it. He is the most enchanting creature!"

Once Meli forgot to ask Corbet to raise the drawbridge against Champion's venturing off. The kitten was hiding behind a barrel when Siegmond the gander waddled into the courtyard, honking loudly, six wives in a phalanx behind him. He paused, stretched his long neck, head downward, a pose his wives copied. Bayard blinked. The kitten yawned. Champion sat down in imitation of the Fur Knight, his forelegs sticking out straight, but with his head goose-high. He and the gander touched noses. Champion rose, swished his tail, nickered, and began to circle the courtyard. He was followed by one dog, one kitten, one gander, and six geese. Slowly at first, then at a trot, at a canter, at full gallop, at full gallop the line moved (the geese flying briefly

to keep up), and how long it would have circled the courtyard had there been no interruption is anybody's guess. But when two cows peered through the arch, the roar of human laughter that greeted them gave the courtyard creatures pause. The phalanx of geese landed in a perfectly-synchronized folding of wings. The furred ones stood still.

"The Creatures Bow to Him"

That evening, Meli's last before her move to the new round tower, Papa came into her room. The big walnut chest was being packed. But Papa did not watch her fold her many gowns, nor Maman putting them away. His eyes were on Champion who was now resting against Bayard on the verbena-strewn floor by the bed. It was rare indeed for Papa to return so early from the hunt and he was still clad in heavy leather garments. In fact his arms and legs squeaked when he moved.

"It seems I missed quite a performance today, Meli. That is quite a colt you have, quite a colt. Corbet's lad rode all the way to tell us about it. The entire château talks and soon the whole valley will if this continues." Papa scratched Champion gently between the ears, then exhaled as if relieved. "Exactly what color are his eyes?"

"I do not know, Papa. It depends on where he is. Moss-green sometimes, gold at others, and against the new brown silk of your canopy-overhung chair, bright blue."

In the silence, Papa and Maman exchanged glances.

"And all animals like him?" Papa asked.

"So it would seem, though I have not yet taken him beyond the drawbridge. Certainly the farm animals and the watchdogs do, and even Siegmond and his geese. Why, Siegmond bowed to him!"

"Hmmmm," said Papa. His eyes fell on the little pile of crystals that gleamed through the herbs on the white-washed floor. He stared. "Salt, Melisande?"

She rose, slammed the lid of the salt-box chair, and with fumbling fingers slid the key into the lock.

"It is my doing," Maman said. "I permitted her to open the salt-box chair, Louis. She wanted so to give these two a treat."

"Salt is terribly expensive, you know."

"Maman knows that, Papa," Meli broke in. "So do I. But he loves it so! Bayard too! I will make it up by not taking any salt for weeks, I promise."

"No, my child. It is not wasteful to treat a guest nor his guardian. Tell me, Daughter, does your little friend take pleasure in his reflection? Does he enjoy seeing himself in your mother's new hand-mirror?"

"O yes, Papa! How did you know? I hold it up for him and he stares and stares."

"So that is where my mirror went!"

"Yes, Maman. Are you very angry? Already it is in my tower room, waiting."

"It is indeed for I have only just seen it." Papa chuckled. "Your mother's new mirror is there, along with the new cushions and the embroidered draperies intended for the South Hall. And Oncle Geoffroi's painting which is missing from the Middle Hall.

29

No doubt when you finish that embroidery of yours the little beast will have my new cushion for his head. Is that not so?"

Before Meli could reply, her parents had departed arm-in-arm, laughing softly, the long boots and spurs Papa had not yet had removed from his legs squeaking with each step.

"Just the same, Louis," Maman said, "this has gone on too long; the child is in for heartbreak. Louis, do you think the colt could possibly be . . ."

"...a most enchanting little horse," Papa said, ending the sentence firmly on a downward lilt.

They had reached the bedroom where Papa was now seated on a stool. The squire began removing the long boots from Papa's legs. As he placed them on the floor, the clank of spurs against stone hid Meli's footsteps as she hid herself behind the door. Perhaps it was wrong to listen but there were times when children must spy to protect those whom they loved. This thought, so new and clear in mind, was highly reassuring.

Papa dismissed the squire. Meli held her breath as he passed the door, bumping the leather hunting garments against it. When his step grew faint, she dared breathe again.

". . . for the animals are totally unafraid in his presence and play with him," Maman was saying. "Also, our entire hive of bees flew into the courtyard yesterday and suspended itself a finger's length from his face. He did not so much as blink. When they rested on his head and neck, he gave his happy whinny which we all know by now, all but you who are seldom around. Surely such behavior is unusual?"

"Agreed. But Champion is an unusual little colt, Blanche. I

have never disagreed with that, my dear."

"And it is usual for creatures to bow to a baby beast?" Maman's dark eyes flashed. "I tell you, Louis, the creatures bow their heads when they first meet him. Some, like Bayard, continue to do so. He bows whenever he returns to Champion's side, even if he has left him for the briefest spell. Now tell me, just how usual is that?"

Papa shrugged, then gave an unconvincing laugh. "Well, we all know our Bayard. Our children are not the only ones who think of him as the Fur Knight. Now if it were the stallion, Galpin's Tonnerre . . ."

"Tonnerre has been with Champion exactly once. Galpin told me that as he walked up to his horse carrying the colt, Tonnerre lowered his head in an unmistakable bow."

"I thought Tonnerre licked the colt. So Galpin told me."

"And so he did. But he licked him after he bowed."

"Could this not be coincidence?" Papa plucked at Maman's lute. The notes were slow, pensive ones and uncertain.

"Perhaps," Maman replied. "It is Galpin's story; it is Melisande's. But even if it is mere fabrication on the children's part, have you not heard and seen enough to give you pause? What about the touch-me-nots, those purple flowers whose leaves go to sleep and shrivel at the touch? Why is it this creature can nuzzle them and they do not move? Why is it that for him only they do not follow their nature and, like tiny springs, shrink back to near-nothing? Yes, Louis. This I have seen for myself. Champion was by the west wall where grows the biggest bush of touch-me-not. He sniffed them and made little soft sounds as if he were telling them something agreeable and not a one of them drew

31

back, not a one. Now explain that if you can!"

Papa's jaw had dropped. He folded his arms across the gold and green of his linen shirt. There was a deep frown on his face.

"All right, my dear. You win. It is indeed time we consulted Elvine."

Unicornity Tests

"Galpin, just who is Elvine?" Meli asked the next morning over their breakfast of bread and ale. She was always hungry after chapel.

"A cousin of the Count's and a real bore. But she is said to have known a wise woman who taught her things unknown to most—the magic of herbs and spells, for instance."

"A witch?" Meli choked.

"If so, a white one which means she is on the side of Good. They say she can give unicornity tests."

"Unicornity tests? Are they painful?"

"Of course not, stupid. If you are not going to finish that ale, pass your cup over to me." Without waiting for her to do so, Galpin reached across and grabbed. "Do not look so anxious, little sister. They say the tests do not hurt one bit so your precious Champion has nothing to fear. Our precious Champion; Papa is growing fond of him too."

"You are certain the tests are not painful?"

"Of course I am certain. Stop worrying, Meli!"

But this she could not do. Though Elvine was not coming until Champion had acquired some teeth—these being necessary equipment for at least one of the tests—the delay did not lessen Meli's concern. She knew that once officially identified, Champion would assume an importance she did not wish him to have in the world of adults. He would be less exclusively hers. Beyond this certainty, she did not care to probe. She urged Nanette to continue to listen in whenever her parents talked of her unicorn, and to report everything she heard.

Days passed. It was hot now for jousting and other violent sports. In their place, Galpin worked on indoor subjects in the heat of the day—on the law, and on the proper carving of meat and fowl, a most necessary art for a future squire. Melisande mastered a new song on the lute, made some progress with her embroidery, strove to learn chess under Galpin's rather muddy instructions, and was taught by Maman to make the rose water for the washing of hands before and after meals. These things Meli did while her unicorn slept, for she was now familiar with his routine and the times when he needed sleep.

These last were growing shorter. Champion woke very early once and chose to have the run of the château. Run he did, especially in the Middle Hall where the staff was making ready for the big meal of the day.

"Get that colt out of there," Papa ordered. "Quickly!"

The children did, but not before Champion had tugged at a wall-hanging and pulled it down. It was, of course, the finest and most costly of the tapestries, as everyone remarked.

"He grows strong and frisky," Galpin told Meli. And he was right, for Champion could play for much longer periods now. He was also beginning to teethe. So far, she had been able to con-

33

ceal this fact from others but her room in the new tower was somewhat scarred already, with the polish removed from one of the legs of the canopy-bed, from her *prie-dieu*, and from one corner of her clothes chest. At least Champion was sparing the high-backed oaken chair. Brand-new it was, the first chair she had had and a rare thing indeed, one of perhaps a dozen of its kind in the entire castle, perhaps in the land.

"No, no, no, no! You are not to chew on my chair, do you understand? On the chest if you must and even on the leg of the bed, but not on my chair!"

"What is this Meli? Why are you scolding?" Maman was in the doorway, looking in. "You? Polishing? But how extraordinary! Leave that to Nanette or Germaine, my child. Why are you polishing that corner of the chest anyway?" Maman stepped inside to kneel by the chest. "Ah! Now I understand." She reached out and patted the smaller of the two white beasts. "Teething, are you? This is good news indeed, my little one."

Elvine appeared on Midsummer Eve, one of those nights specially dear to witches. Each member of the de Vrillac family had some fern and walnut leaves on his person but only Meli clutched angelica flowers in her left hand. Of all known herbs, angelica was the most potent against evil spells and witchcraft. Meli drew Champion to her, hiding him with her body, and quickly rubbed the flowers along his mane.

"What a lovely room!" Elvine exclaimed as Papa closed the door. They had managed to smuggle her up to the new tower after dark without even Nanette any the wiser.

35

"…new pottery Roman lamp…new parchment panes at the windows…rose curtains to match the spread…. Really, my dear Blanche!" Elvine's voice, rasping and loud, echoed against the walls. "You and Louis do spoil your children so! Even if that creature I see peering behind Melisande is not a unicorn, it is much, much too beautiful for a mere child. But more on this later. Why do you not follow our custom and send your young ones to be trained in other noble households? They are quite old enough." Elvine paused for breath.

So distracted had she been by the words, it was only now that Meli noticed her unicorn had been under observation all through this tirade.

"And here you may be permitting a mere wisp of a girl the care of a uni…"

"Enough, Elvine. Will you please get down to business?" Maman's foot tapped hard against the floor and her mouth was a straight line. "We happen to enjoy our children's presence."

Elvine reached for the chair she had been offered and sat down at last. Papa was seated on a stool, Maman on the bed beside Meli, while Galpin stood guard by the door.

"There are some questions that must be asked, Melisande. Are you prepared to answer me?"

She was, but instinct told her to express less than the whole

·truth. Well yes, Champion did sometimes rest his head in her lap.
…What was that—flower music, rumbling moss? She did not
remember. No indeed, there was nothing unusual about his
eyes…

"Melisande!" Elvine spoke sharply.

…except that they changed color. Perhaps his coat did glow
a bit at night but that was because she brushed it as often as she
did her hair. Bowing animals? She was not sure….

"Unicornity Test Six. Kindly bring me a mirror, young lady."

Meli raised the lid of her chest and glanced quickly at Maman
who had never reclaimed the mirror; she was smiling encourage-
ment. It was a lovely mirror of highly polished silver and a pleasant weight in the hand. Instantly, Champion was by her side,
peering into it.

Elvine snorted. She sounded so very like a horse that Champion
whinnied in return. "Aha! Aha! He does indeed admire his reflection."

"Would you not too if you were beautiful?"

"Melisande de Vrillac! Your manners!"

She looked into the mirror. Her gray eyes were wider than
usual and the color in her cheeks matched the deep rose of her
new gown. The gown had a lace bodice like Maman's, and the
new pleated sleeves. A matching cap partly concealed her hair
which was wound in a dark thick braid over each ear. Champion's
head, so close to hers right now, sported a bow of the same deep
rose. Galpin had said it looked ridiculous but he had been wrong.
Nothing could make Champion look ridiculous. He was beautiful and for the moment his eyes matched hers.

39

"Truffles," said Elvine loudly. "Unicornity Test Seven."

"I beg your pardon?" Papa said.

"I said 'truffles,' Louis. Please send for a few truffles. And have you one silver salver and one gold salver of about equal size?"

Papa looked very doubtful.

"Of course we do," Maman answered. "But it is hardly the truffle season, you know, Elvine. Pigs dig for those delectable and rare mushrooms around Christmas and we have but one oak near which they grow."

"No truffles, then," said Elvine. "We shall…"

"I did not say that we had none, Elvine. Come here, please, Galpin, and I shall tell you where to find them. Also the salvers."

"And some ordinary mushrooms as well, child," Elvine ordered. Galpin opened the door. "One moment, please! Walnuts too. We shall also need walnuts, my child."

"But they too are out of season!" Maman sounded quite cross. "What we have left will be rather stale."

"No matter, no matter whatsoever. Bring the walnuts as well, my child, shell them, and remember to be quiet and not rouse the servants."

Galpin drew himself to his full height and more. "Is there anything else you will require?" he asked.

The waiting seemed interminable. When Galpin did reappear, Elvine placed the shelled walnuts on the chest, put three truffles in the gold salver and three ordinary mushrooms in the silver one. She placed both salvers on the green and yellow mosaic-tile floor where the flames from the wall-bracket candles were reflected in the metals.

"The silver shines, so does the gold. Now watch." She paused. "Test Eight. A unicorn will seek out the rarest food on the most lordly dish."

Without a moment's hesitation, Champion trotted over to the gold tray, whinnied with joy, lowered his head, and gulped. The truffles were gone. He did not give the silver tray so much as a second glance.

"See that?" Elvine sounded positively triumphant.

"What does that prove?" Galpin whispered in Meli's ear. "We already knew Champion prefers the best."

"I have yet to see a *horse* show interest in truffles," Papa was saying.

Elvine reached for the walnuts on the chest. "Or in these. Have you ever known a horse to have a veritable passion for walnuts? Watch this. Test Eight."

"No, nine," Galpin corrected.

"Unicornity Test Nine." Again, something unspoken and invisible passed between Elvine and Champion. He came to her at once, unhesitatingly. The walnuts disappeared before she had time to set the dish on the floor. Champion licked his chops, licked the dish, then whinnied loudly enough to rouse the sleepiest sentinel. He pranced. He swished his tail. "There, there." Elvine patted him on the forehead. "Do you see what I mean? They always love walnuts with a passion."

"So do I," Galpin said. "But that does not make me a uni..."

"Galpin, that is enough!"

But Galpin would not be stopped. "I still believe the only way to know a unicorn from a non-unicorn is by noticing whether it

41

has a single horn in the middle of its forehead. Meli's colt does not."

"That is enough, Galpin!"

Papa's words were drowned under the stamping of Elvine's right foot as she halted before the boy. No small woman to begin with, she seemed to have grown taller yet. In a voice that was menacingly even and flat, she asked Galpin what knowledge he had of the world unseen and proceeded to tell him some of hers. As she spoke, a picture grew ever more vivid in Melisande's mind —of Elvine collecting herbs so rare few had even heard the names, collecting these by the light of the full moon or just before sunrise, then going to a thatched hut (such as a serf would dwell in, without a floor and windowless) to brew queer mixtures and murmur incantations. It was not a pleasant picture. The bedroom was full of eerie forces that could be felt though not seen. Meli would place a bouquet of St. John's herbs over her bed tonight to ward off evil dreams and spirits, a bouquet of fern, purslane, fennel and St. John's wort, for all were protectors from witchcraft. And she would place another such bouquet in the fresh balm she had strewn on the tiles for the white creatures to sleep on.

"...impossible to give Test Eleven," finished Elvine.

"Ten," Galpin said. Both Papa and Maman glared at him.

"Ten *and* Eleven are water-conning tests," said Elvine, apparently unperturbed. "As I have said, the alicorn or horn of the unicorn is a detector of poison and a cure for it. As a matter of fact, the alicorn cures many ills. If your creature were older, we could for instance file a bit of powder from the alicorn and feed it to one of two poisoned pigeons. The one fed the powder would

survive the arsenic, the other who had been given the arsenic without the powder would die."

"Oh." Meli hugged Champion closer. In her mind's eye she could see him more grown up, dipping his horn into a stream and ridding it of poisons simply by so doing. Elvine had had a copy made of a priest's eyewitness account of such a scene in the Holy Land. She would lend the de Vrillacs the manuscript.

"You could, of course, try dipping this little fellow's whole head in poisoned water…"

"Never! I will not permit any…" Meli began.

"…but I would not advise it. That particular power may not be his until the alicorn has grown in." Elvine reached over and tweaked Champion's ear, a familiarity he did not seem to resent in the least. "Fine little fellow!" she cooed. "Splendid specimen of genus *Unicornis Guyennius*, our local species. How clever of you not to have your horn at birth like *Unicornis Artus!*"

Papa leaned forward on the wooden stool. "Are you saying what I think you are, Elvine? Are you saying this colt *is* a unicorn?"

The stillness became intense. When Elvine chose to reply, her voice was as emotionless as if she had been discussing spinning or a new embroidery stitch. But her eyes gleamed.

"My dear Louis, there can be no doubt, no doubt whatsoever. It is obvious that here in our beloved Guyenne, the unicorn young are different and develop rather slowly. It may be four or five months yet before the horn grows in. And when that occurs —and it will—may God help you. The whole land will learn of the so-called colt your daughter has been tending!"

45

One could hear breathing, so quiet it was. Galpin leaned over to pat the Fur Knight.

"Melisande," Elvine spoke gently, "you might wish to add a slim collar of mountain ash, as is the custom in Artusland. Angelica is fine but rowan is infallible. Did you pick your bouquets while walking backwards and did you pick them from parish grounds?"

"I did."

"Good." Elvine rose. "If ever you have reason to believe he has been cursed, just trace a circle around your unicorn and have him cross it. He will then be unbewitched. May God help you!"

Champion at the Yearly Feast

Though Maman tried to make her believe that Elvine's last remark was just "her manner of speaking, one of Elvine's little ways of being impressive," Meli was unconvinced. More than that, she was afraid. How stupid she had been not to have allowed everyone to think Champion was just another baby horse, beautiful to be sure, the most beautiful ever, but still a horse.

"Maybe he would be less noticeable if we dye him," Galpin suggested. Meli was feeding Champion a brew of wine and balm leaves. About his neck was a slim wooden circlet which Galpin had fashioned unasked.

Meli shook her head. "That might be harmful to him; Papa said so. Besides, what good will that do when the alicorn appears? It will be just as evident, no matter what color his coat.—There, there, my little one. Is that better? This wild balm grows in the woods near where we found you and is the very finest for aching teeth.—No, Galpin, dye him I will not. But when he is noticeably a unicorn, why then I shall keep him away from people and in hiding. We shall go out to play only at night."

"And if our parents find out, you will find yourself locked up in your tower, with or without your unicorn. Do you really believe you could keep them from knowing?"

"Only with your help. And help me you will."

Galpin frowned. "What makes you so certain of that?"

"Because you love him too. You would not permit Bayard to guard us so constantly otherwise. You do not wish my unicorn stolen any more than I do."

Nor did her parents, it seemed, for she was told not to let him out of her sight unless family or staff were about. Papa added that a unicorn was a rare and wondrous creature, as if she had not known this all along. He thought hers was the first ever to be raised in captivity. Were there any herbs that Champion liked especially for his bed?

"Why, Papa! He loves them all though perhaps he does show a slight preference for angelica. But he likes thyme, too, and fennel."

Papa nodded. "So it can be angelica, fennel, thyme…" He moved toward the door, then turned abruptly. He was flushed under his tan. "You will say nothing about this talk to anyone, Meli? If you please." His voice grew lower still. "…unicorn… the least a person can do…"

"Papa, I understand perfectly and I will not say a word to anyone."

47

Maman had a word with her later that same day. There was a supply of last year's walnuts which she had collected and hidden in the storeroom of the old square tower. They were behind a barrel and only Maman, Galpin, and now Melisande knew of their existence. On no account was Papa to learn of how they were being used. Did Meli understand?

"May I keep your new hand-mirror, Maman?"

"Of course you may."

"Thank you very much. And I will never mention walnuts to Papa until you tell me I may."

With Galpin's help, she placed the hand-mirror on the chest Champion-high. Over his favorite resting place and low against the stone where a unicorn could admire it, she re-hung Oncle Geoffroi's painting.

Every morning now, the head gardener delivered the finest roses still moist with dew. He had noticed how much Champion loved their scent. Nanette, Lise, Corbet, and one of the squires shyly volunteered they had nice voices and had noticed Champion's love of music. Might they perhaps sing to her accompaniment? The sentinels offered to protect Champion at any time of day or night. Last, but surely not least, Bayard proffered a bone. Old and earth-covered it was, a favorite treasure. Champion graciously chewed on it for the time it takes to burn one candle. The Fur Knight watched, enraptured.

"You are spoiled, spoiled, spoiled," Meli said. "You are the most spoiled unicorn in all the land."

The summer days were gone. Champion had four teeth. Maman added a daily dose of boiled celery seed to his potion of balm, "against growing pains," she explained. There was talk of perhaps another battle with the English. Papa and Galpin went hunting with their falcons, newly trained, hooded on their wrists.

No outsider had seen Champion since Elvine's secret visit. By unspoken consent, neither the family nor the staff talked of the unicorn outside the castle walls. The yearly feast at which the de Vrillacs honored their overlord, the Sire de Châteauroc, was the occasion on which Champion chose to make his first public appearance.

The overlord and his retinue were at the Great Table, with the Sire de Châteauroc seated in the canopy-overhung chair which Papa yielded only to his superiors. The long oak table was set with a cloth of purest white and with silver salt cellars, spoons, and drinking cups upon it. At the overlord's place was the golden goblet with lid reserved for him, for the King, or other royal guests. Near the goblet was a golden bowl for the Sire de Châteauroc's sole use; everyone else shared one with his neighbor.

"Remember, Meli, only the tips of the fingers in the sauce, please," Maman whispered.

Meli nodded. She was not likely to forget her manners on this, her first time at the Great Table, where only the important sat. The Middle Hall was as full as she had even seen it, with ladies clad in long gowns trimmed with squirrel or sable. Some wore headdresses with broad bands tied under the chin to frame the face. The latter itched a bit, as Meli knew; especially when one was seated near the fire. The knights wore long robes with their arms embroidered upon them and none were more handsome than Papa or his son.

49

Maman had borrowed more help from nearby Château Mireau to assist in preparations; two of these servants now tended the fire. An extra varlet was placed by the wine casks near the tapestry-covered wall. His sole duty was to draw wine as needed.

In the soft light of torch and fire, everything shone that could and the tablecloths were spotless as they would not be once diners used them to wipe lips and hands.

The meal was magnificent. There were roast boar cooked with cinammon, guinea hen, squab, venison, and peacock, each flavored intriguingly with one of the new spices brought from the East. There were jellies of swan, followed by figs, pears, and apples, walnuts and almonds, all but the figs from the de Vrillac lands. The talk bored Melisande for it was of chain-versus-plate armor, and the crossbows the English were heard to use, and whether these were to be of lasting value as a weapon. Once the overlord called out to Meli that he heard she had a new little colt. The venison slipped from her fingers to the floor where one of the dogs snapped it up. Before Meli could think what to reply, Papa was saying what a charming little thing it was, though not as fine as Galpin's stallion, and would his lord not care to try some pepper with the peacock?

"An exquisite feast, Louis," said the Sire de Châteauroc later as he wiped his hands on the tablecloth. "Never have I had such food."

"Our crops have been especially splendid this year," Papa said.

The Sire de Châteauroc licked fig juice from his fingers and leaned back in the canopy-overhung chair. "So I have heard, Louis. There have been rumors so preposterous I shall not pass them on. I hear your walnut crop is such as to take one's breath away; nothing like it anywhere. And may I repeat what should be pleasing to your ears: Your wine...ah, your wine." He sipped. "It is magnificent. Outstanding." He sipped again. "Extraordinary! Just what is it that you are doing to your vines of late?"

Papa was spared the necessity to reply. The overlord bent his head slightly and raised the gold goblet. It never did reach his lips. A warm weight pressed his arm. Something soft, white and furry hid the goblet from view. He heard lapping.

"What, but what..." he began.

Meli leapt to her feet. "Champion! Champion! Stop that at once. My lord, he is only a baby colt who knows no manners." Meli tried not to think of the dreadful things that were done to disrespectful vassals. "Please do not have him executed, please!"

"What an idea! Of course not, little Melisande." The Sire de Châteauroc chuckled as he caressed the slim white neck. He had not moved the goblet. Champion did not lift his head until he had lapped the last drop. He nuzzled the overlord's hand.

"You raise your future mount on wine?" asked the overlord as he went on patting. "How becoming that bow is to him, Melisande."

"Oh no, my Lord. But he is teething so we serve him his dose of brewed herbs this way."

"How very original! The de Vrillacs have always spoiled their beasts outrageously, have they not, Blanche?"

Maman smiled back. "I cannot say that I agree. But there is no doubt our family is kind to creatures."

"Because of Geoffroi, of course." The Sire de Châteauroc did

51

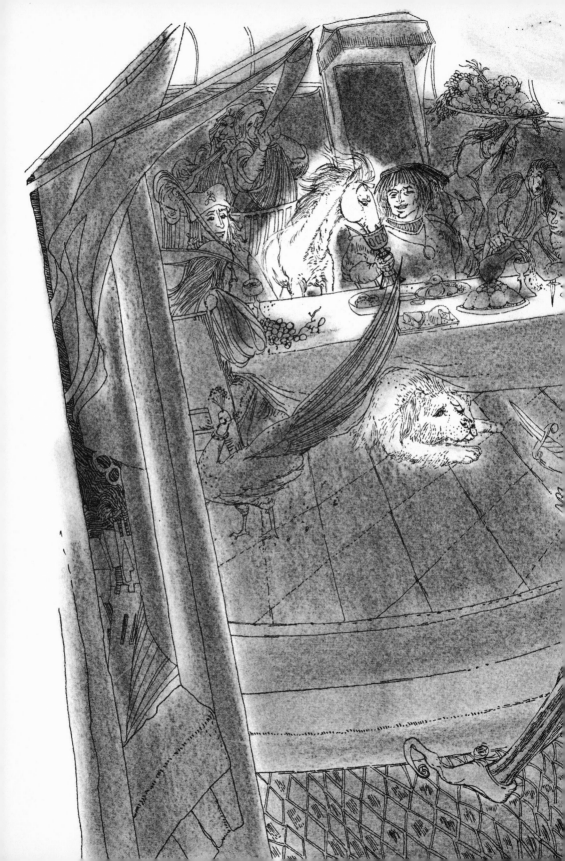

not look up as he was now studying Champion intently. So was his unexpected guest—an envoy from the King, no less—whose arrival had required a change in seating plans.

"Fine man your brother was, Louis, and born with a special love for beasts. Do you still have that magnificent Great Pyrenee, Bayard? You know, this is truly an exceptional little colt, the only perfect one I have ever beheld. If the secret is the serving of wine, then I shall start imitating you tomorrow." With one hand, the Sire de Châteauroc scratched Champion behind the ears. With the other, he raised the white head so that he could look into the eyes.

The King's envoy, one Nicolas Legrand, still sat with his gaze fixed on the unicorn. He had not said a word.

"Perhaps, when this little horse is too big for your daughter to play with, you will consider selling him to me, Louis."

"Perhaps."

"I would pay well. In fact, I am willing to do so right now." The Sire de Châteauroc leaned forward. "Four thoroughbred colts imported from Araby. I have just received them and will trade all four for this one. An unheard of bargain for you, no?"

"No," said Papa gently, shaking his head from side to side. It was so quiet at this end of the Great Table that the cracking of a walnut could have been heard. "Champion belongs to my daughter," Papa said.

"I see. Well, what would you say to such a trade, little Melisande?" The Sire de Châteauroc's voice was light and teasing but his eyes belied the tone, as did his hand which had never left the unicorn's head. From under the table Bayard began to growl,

55

then stopped suddenly at Galpin's command.

"Never." Meli's voice broke. "Never would I agree to such a thing. I shall fight until death if necessary."

There was laughter. The Sire de Châteauroc guffawed and slapped his knee with a smack so loud that Champion started, slipping from under the overlord's grasp. He stood still for the span of a flame's flicker. Then he leaped. He leaped high over Papa's head, over the Great Table, over the King's envoy who was seated across from his host. The diners gasped. For a moment they froze—one with hand halfway to mouth, another with goblet upraised. Did a rainbow really mark the path of that leap? Meli wondered. Or was it some trick of reflected torch and firelight? Her unicorn was by her side now where she could hug him safe.

"That was not possible," said the overlord. He reached down for his fallen knife before the squire could do so. His voice was low and grave. "No colt could do that. Nor could a full-grown horse."

"How very right you are." Papa raised his goblet. "We were all dreaming. We must have shared a common dream caused by this wine you praise so highly. Champion has never taken such a jump before nor did he now. Our minds tricked us."

"Indeed." The Sire de Châteauroc stared hard at the furry white forehead now across the table from him and at Meli's right. "Were there not something lacking from that little colt's head, I would say the de Vrillacs had nothing less than a unicorn in their possession."

"And I would agree." The King's envoy spoke for the first time since introductions had been made and it was perhaps this fact that gave such weight to his words, for all the diners turned his way. "There is no nobler beast than the unicorn, none more able to inspire courage and daring. How greatly a unicorn would help the King's cause!"

"It is a well-known fact that his horn rids any drink of poison," said one of the overlord's retinue.

His neighbor smiled. "Just think how safe a unicorn owner would be with one around."

"What about the royal taster?" asked someone with laughter in his voice. "What wouldn't a unicorn mean to him! Why, tasters have been known to die in sampling royal food and drink."

The King's envoy squeezed two walnuts with one hand until one of them cracked. "The alicorn alone is worth a fortune, you

59

know. Why, the whole beast is claimed to be medicinal. It is said that a belt of the skin will protect one from fever, and that boots of the same give immunity from plague."

What more if anything the King's envoy had to say on the subject Meli did not wish to hear. She had risen abruptly, pleading illness, and had run from the Middle Hall with Champion and Bayard at her heels.

The Overlord Promises Protection

"The Sire de Châteauroc knows," Galpin told Melisande later. "Even if that envoy does not. But the overlord is our cousin who has known us all our lives, and he is an honorable knight. Such a man would neither betray nor steal your unicorn. Let us ride off tonight and beg his protection."

This proved unnecessary. When the moon was high, hoofs sounded on the path leading to the drawbridge. As the lone figure pulled to a halt, he was seen to be none other than the Sire de Châteauroc himself, clad in thick woolen stuff such as peasants wear and with plain sword at his belt, with no jeweled baldric or hilt to catch the moon's cold gleam.

"Cousin Pierre," said Papa softly, using the greeting he saved for private occasions.

"Yes, Louis. I must speak with you and your family right now."

And on the lowered drawbridge, in voice too soft to be overheard by the sentinels, the Sire de Châteauroc offered protection.

"I must not tarry. I wish none of my household to know of this visit. But if you..." He paused. "If your—and I dare not say the name, for if I did I should be obligated to report so unusual a presence to the King—if your colt should need protection, if you should wish him hidden, for instance, please call on me." He smiled warmly at Melisande. "I would give much to own the beast myself as you well know. But I shall be satisfied to have him the property of cousins. Remember. Call on me when you need help. I will do all I can, and everything I can."

The Sire de Châteauroc was tall and fair in the moonlight and his bearing courtly despite the rude garments. Never had Meli loved him more than at that moment.

"Your father serves me better than well," he was saying. "But it is not just for his loyalty that I would guard the——" he caught himself——"the colt. A more wondrous beast was never born in our Guyenne nor in any other land. And now I would speak with you men, Louis and Galpin."

The ruse they planned there in the moonlight proved successful. Rumor was spread the next day of Champion's death. When the King's envoy arrived unannounced at Château Vrillac, he found the family mourning. Meli was sent from the room when he asked to see the body. Nanette told her later that Papa and Galpin had produced a dead white colt so like Champion in build and size that she had nearly cried out. The envoy had stared a moment and tears had actually come to his eyes.

"How horrible. Where did they find it?"

Nanette would only shrug in reply, and mutter something about Elvine, and how the men had ridden through the night until they found her and secured her aid. (The colt had been a brown one until she turned him white.)

As the days passed, so did the sense of menace and the memory of that fateful feast. Champion took to whimpering if rubbed on the forehead. He was growing in length, and he was up to Meli's chin in height. One morning she woke to see a tiny, rounded pyramid growing from the hard spot on his forehead. No bigger than her little finger it was, thicker at the base, of purest white, and twisty. As Meli stared at it, words she had hoped forgotten echoed in her mind: "*The alicorn alone is worth a fortune....A belt of the skin will protect one from fever...boots of the same give immunity from the plague.*"

"You could file it down, maybe," Galpin suggested, his tone unenthusiastic. "This is done sometimes with long-horned cattle."

"But he is not long-horned cattle, stupid!"

"You silly girl, did I say he was? I was trying to think of ways to conceal his identity. It could be filed down, and perhaps one could take some of Bayard's long white fur to cover the bare spot, paste it on with resin, maybe."

Meli shook her head. "Thank you, but the idea does not please me."

"Nor me. The world is bound to learn of your unicorn, Meli. He cannot be kept a secret forever." Galpin tossed a freshly-shelled walnut to the waiting unicorn, who nuzzled him gratefully in return. The daily chore of shelling was not unpleasant for Champion always expressed appreciation. He neighed joyfully as the children reached into the sack and withdrew a handful of nuts apiece.

"...the crop is so prodigious." Galpin was saying. "I hear the Sire de Châteauroc is sending over some serfs today to help pick them. To help with the grapes, too, and all the other foods. Our land was never poor but now it is fantastically productive. He will take a third of the produce and we shall still have far more than the fief can use."

"That is good.——No, darling Fur Knight, you need not struggle with another walnut. We know you do it only to please Champion.——As I was saying, that is good."

Galpin looked at her thoughtfully. "Is it really? At this rate, we shall be the talk of the entire country. Just how long do you believe our people and the overlord's will hold their tongues?"

"They gain from keeping still, do they not? All the food they can eat and extra to store against famine. So easily come by, too, since there is so much."

"O Meli, what a fool you are! Word will leak out anyway. Especially now that he is visibly a unicorn. From now on, he had better be exercised only by moonlight or starlight when folk may conclude they have dreamt him."

It seemed like good advice. Often, Papa and Maman would dismiss the guards to accompany the children and the two white creatures themselves. None of them would ever forget the moonlit romp of dog and unicorn on Champion's favorite terrain, the clearing in the forest high above the spur on which the château sat. Sometimes, wild things would come from the woods—deer and rabbit and once, a wolf—to join in games the rules for which were never altogether clear to humans. The onlookers grew in number, with the overlord as first addition, then staff from Châteauroc as well as Vrillac.

Meli no longer tied a bow to Champion's mane though she still brushed it. When he wished to be alone at times, she learned to respect his need. She would join Maman, knowing Bayard was on guard at the entry to the tower.

An Encounter With Brigands

Shortly before Christmas, Papa and Maman went to dine at Châteauroc while the de Vrillac servants held a party of their own, with all but the two guards assigned to Champion in attendance. The children set off for a moonlit ride on Tonnerre, with Champion and the Fur Knight trotting by their side, and the guards bringing up the rear. The night was unusually soft and balmy. The clearing in the forest shone with an unearthly light.

Galpin pulled the stallion to a halt and peered over his shoulder. "Strange. The guards are no longer at our heels. I cannot even see them. Can you, Meli?"

"No. There is no sign of them behind us, or elsewhere. They have never been out of sight before, never."

"Well, no matter. They will catch up with us. I shall be obliged to scold them as their orders are not to leave us for a moment." Galpin did not sound altogether sorry at the prospect. Meli pulled her cloak closely about her. She listened for the sound of hoofs that did not come.

Suddenly, the Fur Knight snarled. He bared his teeth and Tonnerre pawed the ground. A wild boar stepped from the forest, his two tusks gleaming as he moved toward them. He paused. He

bowed to Champion. The two of them departed at a trot, heading for the trees. When they reached them, the unicorn turned his head and whinnied an invitation.

"Come back, Champion! Come back at once!" Meli cried.

He did not move.

"Oh, come on, Meli; let us follow them. We need have no fear of the boar with Champion around. And if we did, I have my dagger." Galpin pulled it from its sheath. "You stay here with Tonnerre, Bayard, and warn us if anybody comes this way. Good boy. Our fine Fur Knight."

Dagger in hand, Galpin led the way to the trees. They had covered but a short distance before they found Champion at the foot of a huge oak. Beside him, the wild boar was digging fast, and grunting with excitement. There was something in his mouth when he raised his head, and he dropped the object at Champion's feet. The latter whinnied joyously.

"A truffle!" Galpin cried. "Why, he's showing us a new truffle oak!"

The boar uncovered more of the precious food. Meli fed some to her unicorn, collected the rest. Galpin marked the tree with his dagger. The two creatures moved on and again the children followed, laughing now from sheer delight. When the moon was lower in the west, Galpin had marked eleven more oaks and Melisande carried a cloakful of truffles by the right hand.

There was barking, urgent, sharp. A horse neighed in fury. The way back to the clearing was very long, even under Champion's guidance. From behind the shelter of the trees, the children spied four men trying to approach Tonnerre while he reared and tried to free the rein, and a snarling, snapping Bayard kept them at bay.

"You leave my horse alone!" Galpin cried.

"Well, well, and what have we here? Three young things from Elvenland!" The bigger of the men laughed. He studied the three a moment, then gave a low whistle. "A higher ransom we shall get for these than for the stallion. Think you not so, my friends?"

"Where are our guards? What have you done with them?" Galpin shouted.

"Aye," said the stocky one with legs too short for his body. "A fine ransom we shall get, though whether the overlord will pay more for the son than for the daughter is anybody's guess."

The third one took a step toward Champion. "This colt. Look at it! Will you look at this colt, if you please!"

There was silence, followed by the gasp of indrawn breath. With one accord, the men moved toward the trio. Bayard snarled. As the stocky one grabbed Meli by the arm, she screamed, and Bayard hurled himself at the man's throat. The man fell. The wild boar appeared from behind a stump, grunting with rage, his head low, his tusks lethal as the sharpest lance and gleaming in the moonlight. He charged. With a scream of terror, the men fled.

"Quick!" said Galpin. He had untied the rein from the tree and held Tonnerre with one hand, Meli with the other. Together, and with the white creatures following, they ran for the safety of the forest. "Brigands," Galpin panted. "Will come back. Soon. For Champion especially."

They moved fast, at a near run. Champion had taken the lead

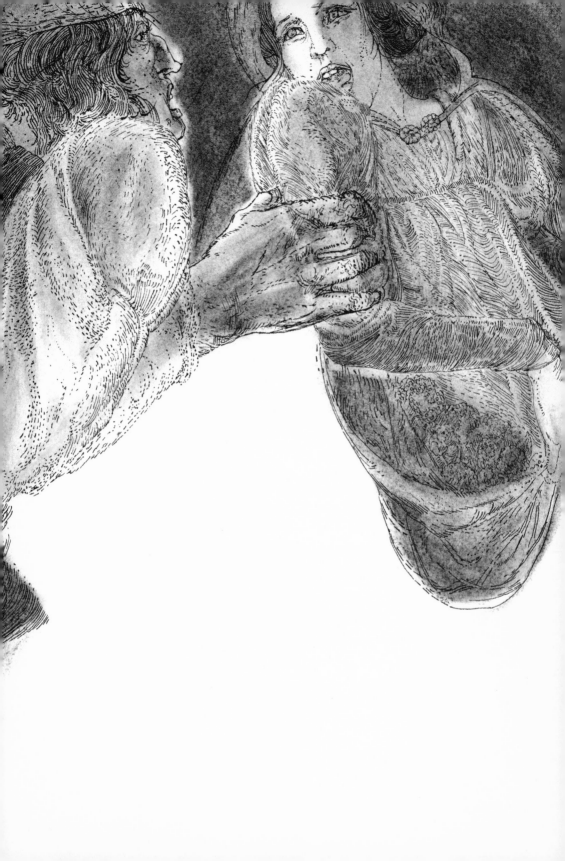

and the glow of his white coat made him easy to see. The mountainside was steep and the earth springy underfoot. So thick were the trees that Meli wished she had a torch; twigs brushed her face, sometimes struck her, and she kept her eyes half-closed to protect them. She tripped.

Galpin yanked her to her feet. "Careful, Meli!" He turned to the dog. "No growling, Fur Knight. That would give us away."

Already, they could hear their pursuers below. In their anger they must have forgotten how far voices carry upward, for each word of the argument was clear. Jack should have slain the dog at once, berated one of the men; only a fool would believe he could deflect one of that breed from his guard duty.

"Hush, you simpletons!" cried another. "Straight ahead and up to the right a bit. Yes, over there. Those two white spots are the beasts. Remember, we can lose the others if we must, but not the unicorn!"

Closer yet the hunters came. Champion had to search now for spaces wide enough for Tonnerre to pass. Meli felt a warm tongue on her hand; it was Bayard. He was between her and Galpin, and now he was licking his master's hand. He was trotting off to the left, fast, but no faster than would be possible for humans. Meli opened her mouth.

"No, do not call him, Meli. 'Tis an old sheepdog's trick Bayard is using. To get them off our scent. Remember, he could run. Faster than man."

The three brigands had spotted the Fur Knight. They could not see the other white creature, for Tonnerre hid him from view. "Left, I think," said the leader. "Always follow the white."

75

Champion had found a space among the trees wide enough for the stallion's body. They were now on the steepest part of the cliff. It was a stony, sandy area, with patches of juniper. Even without Champion, they must be clearly visible in the bright moonlight.

"Up there, look! There they are!" cried one of the men.

"Curses on that dog!"

"Hurry."

The other side of the cliff was moonless and so dark by sudden contrast that Galpin took Champion's tail in the hand that also held the stallion's rein, and pushed Meli behind him. No noise did they make now, for their feet trod on stones which were often sharp and painful. As their eyes became adjusted, they saw a blackness not far below. It was the beginning of the northern forests. They stretched onward as far as the eye could see.

Meli's side hurt. She was still clutching the cloak with the truffles. Galpin breathed in shallow gasps.

"I cannot go farther," Meli whispered.

"But we must," Galpin urged.

They were on a small ledge when Champion made the sharp turn into the mountain itself. The cave was hidden by the scrub pine which grew in single file along the opening, the branches concealing its width which was just sufficient for the passage of a full-grown horse. As Meli helped pull Tonnerre in—he was reluctant to enter so eerie a place—a large white something sped under his body and rubbed against Galpin's thighs. Both children cried out.

"The Fur Knight!"

76

"Most beautiful one. Our Bayard, brave and bold. Darling, dear, beloved Bayard..."

"Meli, hush! I can hear them coming over the top."

Champion nickered almost inaudibly for their attention. Deeper and deeper he led them, until they could see naught but the white coats of the two beasts, the one leading, the other at the rear. Beneath their feet was water up to Meli's ankles. It was a very cold running stream. The walls were so close they could be touched with ease. Drops of dampness oozed from them. Overhead, water dripped intermittently and with a kind of diabolical malice, landing each time between collar and bare neck. It would then slither down, causing the boy and girl to shiver and Meli to squeal as well. She squealed without fear of being overheard, for they had been walking inside the mountain now long enough to say many prayers.

"What a horrible place! Must we stay in here, Galpin?"

"Yes, until Champion leads us back. But we do not have to walk farther, Meli. See? He has stopped now. We are safe." Galpin sighed heavily and felt the walls with care. "Very cold, and damp enough to rain. I did hope he could find us a dry spot for resting. We cannot even lean here."

"Do you think they will follow us?"

She could sense the shaking of his head from side to side. The men would assume their prey had reached the northern forests and would be heading for them.

"I hope you are right. Oh Galpin, the Fur Ones are frightened. Feel how they tremble. Even more than I do."

"It is only the cold," Galpin replied. "Could I but see the

77

height of this cave, I would lift you to Tonnerre's back to keep you dry and warmer. But it is so dark I cannot judge whether there be one hand's or one thousand hands' space between him and the rock above."

"Thank you. But it is for Champion that I worry. There are evil things about. And a terrible noise of rushing water like the wailing of many giants, a noise most pleasing to cave dragons."

"More like the sound of that loud Elvine taking a bath," Galpin joked. "There is nothing to fear, though the place be horrid. Your imagination works too well, little sister."

"Just the same, I hear the water rushing in great sorrow." Meli hugged the White Ones to her, holding them close. "Against me Champion shivers, and the Fur Knight is shaking too. There is a wild gleam in Tonnerre's eye."

"You cannot see his eye, much less any gleam. The white coats, yes, but nothing more." Galpin's voice was steady. "The sorrow is not the water's but your own for you believe yourself to be at fault."

"What do you mean?"

"Just that. Yet how could you have done otherwise? The unicorn was but a baby and a waif when found; none but a heartless soul would have left him there to die. You could not have known then that he would be a fortune-hunter's dream and a prize for all to covet." Galpin reached for and found her hand. He squeezed it hard. "Drop those silly truffles and put on your cloak," he said.

She ignored the order. "Is he growing very fast?"

"Very. No horse ever grew so fast. He would be quite able to fend for himself now."

Meli shivered. Another icy drop slid down her neck but this time she did not squeal. Champion lowered his head, dipped his horn in the stream, and drank.

"I had forgotten my thirst," remarked Galpin after they had all done the same. "I feel much stronger now. And a good thing, since your unicorn would lead us farther. After him, Meli."

It was not another endless journey but a matter of perhaps one hundred paces, most of them uphill. When Champion stopped, there was no icy stream beneath their feet. Nor were there walls of sweating stone to be touched by outstretched hand.

"Thank you, Champion," Galpin said. "Feel how much better this is, Meli? Wider, too, not so oppressive. I do believe he has led us into a wider chamber. We can sit or even lie down. If we huddle together we shall be less cold."

Galpin eased the stallion closer, and himself as well, so that all five were crammed together, warmth from one body spreading to the next, and with it some sense of comfort. Presently they breathed as one. Meli thought the others slept. She herself had fallen into a state somewhere between sleep and wakefulness. She strove not to think of cave demons. The air was heavy and full of evil things, and the need for light was stronger than any hunger pangs. Something brushed against her cheek. To keep from crying out, she stared a while at Bayard to her left, then to her right where Champion lay. He was not asleep after all. She offered him a truffle but he refused it. He brushed his head gently against her arm.

"Are you all right, Melisande?" Galpin asked.

"Not altogether. I am so homesick for light that I can hardly breathe, Galpin!"

"Me too. Never have I loved light more! But it is better to be here than in the hands of brigands; let us remember that and take courage. Champion will lead us out when the time comes. But it will do no harm to say prayers while we wait."

Safe!

Wait they did, until Champion stirred at last. Instantly, the others rose to follow. They walked to what must be the very center of the earth where the darkness seemed greater still. And then—to Meli's inexpressible relief—her feet were wet and cold and she could feel the oozing walls by holding arms out to the sides.

"We are back!" Galpin cried. "He is taking us back the same way, I think."

"Light! It is getting light! I can almost see the color of the walls."

"So can I. Red? Yellow?"

"A sort of orange, they are. Oh Galpin, we can see again, is it not wonderful? Look! We are in a tunnel. How smooth the sides are at the top, and the ceiling. All those lines. Do they mark where the water ran?"

"Perhaps. Meli, I see sky ahead. We have been in the mountain all night and all day, for it is just before sunset."

The speck of golden light grew in size as they went toward it. Champion and Tonnerre neighed and tossed their heads for joy, while Bayard barked his pleasure. Once the group came to a halt. To the right, through a rounded opening, there was a chamber so vast one could not see its end. The floor rose in high, sharp peaks that glistened with moisture. Like a sea of reddish frozen waves it was, with an upside-down sea high above from which hung one tremendous icycle of stone that tapered to a point the width of two thick trees. They shuddered and went on.

"Papa! Maman!" Meli saw them outlined against the light as they came toward the entrance at a run.

"We are safe. Every one of us is safe!" Galpin cried.

Meli was first in Papa's arms, pressed tight against the surcoat, unminding of the armor beneath. Then it was Maman's turn, and the little girl was spun around and passed from one parent to the other. They laughed; they all spoke at once; even the creatures were having their say as Bayard barked and Champion nickered and Tonnerre snorted with relief.

"...guards unharmed," Papa was saying. "But the brigands had tied and gagged them. Why did you two not turn back when you saw you had lost them?"

Meli showed the truffles crushed inside her cloak, and explained about the wild boar, his befriending Champion, and the two of them trotting off toward the tree-line where Champion had paused to whinny his invitation.

"We could not help but follow," Galpin added. "The guards were forgotten in the excitement. Forgive me, please. As the elder, I should have known better."

Papa shook him lightly by the shoulders, so huge was his relief. "I might have done the same at your age. Nothing matters now since the two of you are safe, nothing. Here, take the bread your mother hands you, my son, and you too, little daughter.

81

You have not eaten all day, have you?"

They shook their heads, and each broke off a piece of bread for both dog and unicorn. Meli had never tasted any food as good as that first bite. Then she shared the rest of her portion with the creatures as Galpin was doing.

"Bayard saved us from capture, and it was Champion who found the hidden cave and the long way to it."

"So you have said, Meli. We shall not forget these things. Neither one of them can ever be thanked enough."

It was now the turn of the beasts to be fussed over, to be patted and praised and hugged unashamedly. The trek over the peak and down to the clearing was like play, Meli thought, she was so happy now and so refreshed. She could have walked forever in this company.

"And you actually *stroked* the wild boar?" Maman repeated.

"Indeed yes, did we not, Galpin?"

"Indeed we did. We could not be afraid with Meli's unicorn right there."

"Not my unicorn, Galpin. He belongs to all of us—to you and to Papa and Maman too, and to everyone who loves him."

Good-By, Champion

They had reached that spot from which the Château de Vrillac was at its fairest, where the golden light played with the yellow stone walls, danced on high-peaked and horizontal roofs, and where the liquid diamond that was the moat shone with fairy colors. The new tower stood out in all its freshness.

Meli looked at the young unicorn by her side. He was bathed in gold, still as the poplar on a windless night, and so beautiful in this glow that she dared not reach out to stroke his golden coat.

Hoofbeats sounded. They were muffled by distance. The rider grew in size as he approached, and with him the volume of the gallop. The Sire de Châteauroc was forcing his horse to take the incline at high speed, as a rider does only when he must. Bayard raised his head and howled, a sound so eerie and distressed the sun itself took fear. It sank behind the hills, taking its gold with it, and leaving a light both flat and cold.

Meli stepped forward, dropping Papa's hand.

"Yes, my lord?"

The Sire de Châteauroc gasped for breath, then wiped the sweat from his brow. "Melisande, it is with you I must speak. You see…you see…" He played with the rein, head down.

"I know what you have come to tell me." Meli spoke quietly. "They are after him. Someone has told the King about our unicorn, the fairest unicorn in all the land, and his men are down in the valley below Vrillac, and soon they will search our home if they have not done so already." Meli swallowed.

The overlord would not meet her gaze but kept it fastened on the rein which he was twisting in his hand.

"You have guessed right," he said. "I might hide him at Châteauroc for a day or two, but then…"

"It would solve nothing." Meli hugged Champion to her and buried her face in his soft white mane. "Last night I knew what must be done."

Again she hugged the unicorn, then whispered in his ear. She took a step back and motioned to the trees. "Go," she said softly. "Go quickly, Champion. Go through The Forest, and over the mountain into the northern woods and beyond where no man will give chase. You will be safe then, my darling. Run!"

The Fur Knight whimpered. Overhead, a few stars twinkled. In the gray half-dark, the unicorn seemed to grow in size and whiteness. With a leap of unearthly grace, he turned and raced for the tree-line where he paused, his body half-hidden by the foliage. He looked their way, and all about him there was—what was it Oncle Geoffroi called it?—"a kind of glow." The onlookers crossed themselves and paid him the homage of a bow or curtsey. He bowed back. Then he was gone.

Waiting for their return as Papa had said she would be, stood a little mare with big, dark eyes, and glossy coat of black. She was standing in a bed of yellow crocus by the drawbridge.

84

"Elvine helped choose her from Cousin Pierre's new foals," Papa said. "Can you love her, Melisande?"

"I shall learn to very soon. Thank you, Papa."

Bayard stopped whimpering and wagged his tail. He gave a puppy's yelp of joy.

"The Fur Knight must have a young beast to love, is that not true, Maman?"

"Yes, Meli, it is true."

"And she is a beautiful thing."

"She is the color of my stallion, Meli," Galpin said.

"So she is."

The Fur Knight and the mare had now met and were standing side by side. A nightingale sang overhead. Melisande stepped forward to touch the velvet-soft black nose. She thought she heard a trumpet blast from the crocus near her left foot, but she was not altogether sure.